Isaac Kinley

Labor rhymes

Isaac Kinley

Labor rhymes

ISBN/EAN: 9783337259389

Printed in Europe, USA, Canada, Australia, Japan

Cover: Foto ©Andreas Hilbeck / pixelio.de

More available books at **www.hansebooks.com**

LABOR RHYMES

BY

ISAAC KINLEY.

Upward still, in mighty cycles,
Slowly moves the multitude,
To the final culmination,
Each man's right is all men's good.
—B. S. PARKER.

LOS ANGELES, CAL., April 16, 1886.

INTRODUCTION.

IN GIVING these little poems to the public, I am not foolish enough to pretend indifference to their reception.

"O wad some power the giftie gie us" to look on the bairns of our brains with the eye of the unbiased critic. Not only "It wad frae monie a faut and blunder free us," but save our friends, too, from the infliction of many a foolish book — perhaps mine.

I. K.

O! There be hearts that ache to see
The day-dawn of our victory:
Eyes full of heart-break with us plead,
· And watchers weep and martyrs bleed:
O! Who would not a champion be
In Labor's lordlier chivalry?

Work, brothers mine; work hand and brain;
We'll win the golden age again:
And love's milennial morn shall rise
In happy hearts and blessed eyes.
Hurrah! Hurrah! True knights are we
In Labor's lordlier chivalry.

GERALD MASSEY.

I sing the dawning of a brightness
  Falling on a sleeping world:
Behold upon the eastern mountain,
  Bright the flag of morn unfurled.

I sing of light dispelling darkness—
  Light dispelling fog and mist;
I sing the splendors and the glories
  Of our earth by day-beams kissed.

I sing the earth, an orb of beauty
  Fair reposing in the day;
With all its darkness and its coldness
  Driven by the light away.

I sing its valleys and its mountains,
  And its food-producing soil;
I sing its cities and its hamlets
  Builded by the hand of toil.

I sing of man and sister woman,
  Freed alike from woe and thrall;
For day that in the east is dawning
  Shines with equal light for all.

I sing the time of peace and plenty—
  All mankind a brotherhood—
No mad ambition war is waging—
  Fields of carnage dyed in blood.

Brighter shines the dawning glories
  Of this welcome, breaking day;
How rejoice the toiling millions
  As the clouds and mist give way!

Alike for all this day resplendent
   Shall on land and ocean glow;
And man himself grow truer, nobler,
   For the light his eyes shall know.

Not for the few shall then the many
   Drudge, and trudge, and sweat, and moil,
And of the wealth produced by labor
   None shall rob them or despoil.

The earth shall man's be in its fulness,
   They shall reap alone who sow,
Nor shall they—the toiling millions—
   Hunger in their homes of woe.

Fair Nature spreads her shining treasures—
   Light and air and sea and soil—
And comes she with her crown of glory,
   Binds it on the brow of toil.

No more shall labor crouch a craven,
   Begging for the freeman's right;
But bravely facing unto all men
   Take its own by right and might.

For Right and Might shall stand together
   Married, and the twain be one,
And Right give Might a constant blessing
   For each noble deed that's done.

For on the side of Right shall numbers
  Bravely stand in field or fray;
And from before their forward marching
  Shall the hosts of Wrong give way.

United at the public ballot
  They shall speak with freedom's voice,
And after, with the will of freemen,
  Execute the freemen's choice.

And knowledge then shall come with blessing,
  Labor learn to think and know;
The soul exalted by this knowing
  Into higher beauty grow.

Taught in school of hard endeavor,
  Toiling hand and thinking brain,
Shall toilers learn from wrongs they've suffered—
  Know their rights and dare maintain.

Then shall the workers be the thinkers,
  Workers be the ones of worth,
And plenteous fall in lap of labor
  Choicest blessings of the earth.

No more shall Labor then be crouching,
  Begging for permit to toil;
But Labor be its own employer,
  Labor own the sea and soil.

No more shall crime be running riot,
　Mad and drunk with lust and sin;
But crime that's lawful or unlawful
　Known shall be as things that's been.

And looking forward through the vista
　To the speedy coming time,
No pen shall lend its storied pages
　To ennoble sin and crime.

No inhuman, human butcher,
　Blood-stained fiend of Macedon,
Shall loud be praised in song or story
　For crimes untold and realms undone.

No more shall man delight in slaughter,
　Nor honored be for blood he's spilt;
No more shall honors due to virtue
　Guerdon he that's paid to guilt.

No more shall greatness be in granite—
　Polished pile on pile that's laid—
But wealth that's been from labor plundered,
　Back returned to those who made.

No more be seen the reeling, drunken,
　Hideous making day and night;
No more the greedy sons of Mammon
　Curse the earth with sin and blight.

And no more man shall wrong his neighbor,
  Kneeling base at shrine of Hate;
Sweet Charity the soul elating
  Good for evil compensate.

And everywhere shall honest Labor
  Learn to work with manly pride;
And all the earth with plenty filling,
  Love and joy be multiplied.

Whate'er of good in age called golden,
  Whate'er of beauty poets sing,
Yet more than these, with all their blessings,
  Shall the day that's dawning bring.

Then honored be, shall all who labor—
  All who toil with head or hand—
And proud shall Labor's sons and daughters
  Equal with the highest stand.

See yonder rise the gorgeous palace,
  Of the millions the despoil;
One night within its halls carousing
  Costs ten thousand days of toil.

See! round about it are the hungry,
  Want and woe and wan despair,
What for the weeping and the wailing
  Cares the beast that burrows there?

In all the land the toiling, plundered—
   Victims of his lust and greed—
From early dawn till night they're toiling
   This remorseless wolf to feed.

Not always thus shall be the noble
   Toiling bondsmen to the base;
Not always thus this bestial gorging
   In the life-blood of the race.

Look to the east—the day is dawning—
   Grandly comes the Orient glow;
If thus 'tis beauteous in its twilight,
   What joy the day's full tide to know!

The earth itself shall put on brightness,
   Brighter be the land and main;
And wilderness and desert blooming
   Guerdon be of brawn and brain.

And fairer then shall bloom the garden.
   Sweeter fruits the orchard yield;
And for this dawning, greater harvests
   Come from off the well-tilled field.

About you look and see the glories
   Labor from the earth has won;
Of truth I know that Labor's holy,
   Noble each good deed that's done.

Henceforth, when rise the stately mansions,
  None shall be the price of sin;
But honest work of honest workers—
  Those who build shall enter in.

And brighter still shall come the dawning—
  It shall come the perfect day—
See! Higher waves the flag of morning,
  Brighter are the beams that play.

'Twill be a time of toil and struggle;
  But of toil unmixed with strife;
And from the toiling and the struggling
  All shall grow to higher life.

The noble acts of self-denial,
  Generous deeds for others done—
To house of woe to carry blessings—
  These the proudest laurels won.

Then each shall find his bliss the greater
  For the blessing that he gives;
And man himself shall grow the nobler
  For the noble life he lives.

Oh! Would you hasten on the coming
  Of this bright and beauteous day,
Would you lift your brother, sister,
  Up from out the mire and clay?

If you would mould them to the beauty
  Which their constant souls aspire,
If you would snatch them from the burning,
  Out from the consuming fire;

Then forward is the place of duty;
  Stand a hero at the front,
And bravely in the hour of struggle,
  Of its dangers bear the brunt.

And should you find your brothers, sisters,
  Tired and fainting on the road,
Aweary of the toilsome journey,
  Weary of the heavy load,

Reach out to them the hand of helping,
  Speak unto them words of cheer,
And point them to the light that's dawning
  With its glories coming near.

For we should learn to aid each other
  In the turmoil and the strife—
Should learn to bear each other's burdens
  On the toilsome march of life.

Should learn to bear life's burdens equal,
  Not to shrink from touch of toil,
And gather of the fruits of labor
  From the air and sea and soil.

Or should you find your brother, sister,
  Erring on life's downward way,
Point them to the beauteous dawning
  Gorgeous with the coming day.

'Tis yours to teach of virtue, duty,
  Teach of peace, and love, and truth;
To teach of upright men and women,
  Teach of pure and stainless youth.

For in this time of dawning brightness
  Sin and shame shall flee away,
And love, and peace, and truth, and beauty,
  Grandly glorify the day.

For God will bless the hand of toiling,
  God will bless the soul that's true;
Then faithful in the work we're doing
  Let us walk our journey through.

We dare not silence thoughts we cherish—
  Virtue, beauty, truth and good—
Though we should find that the baptismal
  Font should be a font of blood.

'Tis thus the day I sing is dawning,—
  With each truth that's bravely told,
Still come the day-beams brighter, brighter,
  Bringing blessings manifold.

And in this day we'll walk together,
  Walk with Truth alone our guide;
And in our better, nobler living,
  Be the All-Father glorified.

GOOD NIGHT.

Good night, good night: each mutual friend,
  The members of our faithful band,
Our blessings, each with each, we send,
  As give we each the parting hand.

On what is good we'll ponder well,
  Of all we've seen and heard to-night;
And bound in Friendship's holy spell,
  We'll drink its cup of sweet delight.

We'll keep our pledges faithful, true,
  And help along the generous plan;
We'll honest be in all we do
  And " help each other all we can."

Nor shall we stop and idly wait
  For chance to do a noble deed;
No grudging hand shall hesitate
  When brothers, sisters are in need.

Nor shall we hide our light within
   Our toiling, faithful, noble band,
But others to our order win
   And spread its blessings through the land.

And upward shall our souls aspire
   Unto the purer, nobler love;
And kindle in our souls the fire
   Whose light is of the Light above.

Good night, good night; each mutual friend,
   The members of our faithful band;
Our blessings, each with each, we send,
   As give we each the parting hand.

ASTRÆA.

When hard-hearted Interest first began
  To poison Earth, Astræa left the plain;
Guile, violence and murder seized on man,
    And for soft, milky streams, in blood the riv-
    ers ran.

THOMPSON.

Oh! Why should tears of sadness fall,
  And sorrow's mourning shroud the heart?
Why Avarice spread his deathful pall,
  And make for gold fair Truth a mart?

The heavens spread their lights on high,
  Our earth's aglow with loveliness;
Then why not beaming from the eye,
  And brother's love a brother bless?

It e'en was so in times of eld,
  In fair Astræa's golden reign;
Then man each man a brother held,
  And face that smiled met smile again.

Then virtue reigned, each mutual face,
 As joy it met did joy impart;
The bliss of each to each we trace,
 As heart in kindness spoke to heart.

Ah! Sweet it was, I ween, to see
 The peace and love that friends endear;
The look, the deed of charity—
 The mutual smile, the mutual tear.

Then speech was truth, and guileless thought,
 And none fair Truth did false construe;
Hypocrisy there then was nought,
 And love, oh bliss! on earth was true.

Ne tongue of slander then assailed
 With poisonous breath a brother's fame;
If meed of praise for one prevailed,
 The rival generous owned the flame.

Ne children dug beneath the soil,
 Nor famished mother starved for bread;
Ne stalwart brother begged to toil,
 Nor martyrs then for justice bled. -

And in the early, primal day,
 No need the justice courts impart;
No need of legal rules the sway,
 For thine, O virtue! was the heart.

The bounteous Earth in vernal climes,
  O man, her plenty spread for thee;
Ah! Woe it is in latter times,
  We moil and hunger, thirst and dree.

Astræa, woe it is, thy reign
  Should lose o'er earth and man its sway;
Wilt ne'er resume thy rule again,
  Of peace to glad this latter day?

We ne'er may drink the cup of life
  Filled up with sweetness to the brim,
While peace on earth gives place to strife,
  And lust for gold the heart doth dim.

While man and woman slavish toil
  That they may reap who do not sow,
Must sweat of labor curse the soil
  On which sustaining food must grow.

I pour my scorn, I set my foot
  Upon the low-born lust for gold—
It drags to earth the aspiring thought,
  It drags to hell the aspiring soul.

I would not have within my breast
  The soul corrupt the miser feels,
For all the wealth of Inda blest,
  For all the mines this earth conceals.

I would not yield the free-born will
 And bow to lustful Mammon's spell,
For all the wealth the coffers fill
 Of all the millionaires of hell.

For what's the gewgaw, glittering gold,
 That man should sell his soul to buy?
Exchange the soul, of worth untold,
 For dust that in the earth doth lie.

With groveling thoughts, hell-born he digs,
 In hell-born thoughts his being lives:
With baseness, falsehood, low intrigues.
 The miser for his treasure strives.

Ah! what to him that brother bleeds,
 Or widow's aching heart is wrung?
Ah! what to him are ruthless deeds
 Of bloody crime or perjured tongue?

Ah! what to him that tyrant wields
 The lash upon the toiling slave,
If but the grudging cotton-fields
 The lucre yield his soul doth crave?

Ah! what to him that virgins sell
 Their virgin fame for sister's bread?
Ah! what to him but nought? Till hell
 Shall yield its damned dead,

Shall he ne'er feel for others' woe,
   Nor warm his heart with pity's ruth;
Nor shall his rayless soul e'er know
   The bliss affliction's sigh to soothe.

Oh! when shall earth the brightness see,
   It saw in early primal day?
Oh! when shall gladness fill the ee
   And Love on earth regain its sway?

Not while the soul can worship dust,
   Or wealth with blood its coffers fill;
Not while the low-born, sensual lust
   Shall spread o'er earth its cankering ill.

Not while the base-born lust of gold
   Shall reason hold subordinate;
And pure emotions of the soul
   By passions low be subjugate.

A fairer day shall come I trow,
   Its light shall fall on land and main:
When none shall reap who do not sow,
   And peace on earth resume her reign.

I give, Astræa, homage thee,
   My dreams have oft thy light beheld—
Oh! Shall our earth again e'er see
   The happy days, the days of old?

AMERICA TO EUROPE.

Hail! Ye friends beyond the waters,
   Struggling for dear Freedom's right;
Take our hand—all men are brothers—
   More we pledge you, freemen's might.

Bear aloft your freeman's banner,
   To the eyes of toil unfurled:
Blazon there the noble motto:
   RIGHT AND FREEDOM FOR THE WORLD.

Never more to priest or despot
   Man shall crouch a creeping slave;
Proudly shall he live a freeman,
   Dying fill a freeman's grave.

Bowing meekly to the tyrant
   Only makes his chains more tight;
Never can to masters fawning
   Gain for slave the freeman's right.

Rally 'round your chosen leaders,
  Strive with sword, and tongue, and pen—
This shall be your gathering slogan:
  DOWN WITH TYRANTS, UP WITH MEN.

Tell oppressors, tell them boldly,
  Freedom's sword that's now unsheathed
Never more shall know its scabbard
  While God's air by slave is breathed.

Tell the tyrants, tell them truly,
  Freedom's banner now unfurled
Goes from conquest on to conquer,
  Proudly waving 'round the world.

Tell the despots—make them hear you—
  Rights belong to all alike;
For the wrongs that they have done you,
  You've the power and will to strike.

By the exiles and their sorrows,
  By the tears of loved ones shed,
By the blood of freedom's martyrs,
  They shall bleed for those who've bled.

Not in anger, but in sorrow,
  Hold we out the bitter cup—
Wrong must needs find retribution—
  They must drink and drink it up.

Truth once spoken's truth for ever,
Victor battling with the lie;
Right of all to equal freedom
Not can earth nor hell deny.

Forward is the marching order,
Wrong and falsehood must give way;
As the sun at break of morning
Brings triumphant perfect day.

Ask ye not if slavery's hoary,
Ask not who his minions be;
Truth shall be protecting Ægis—
Bravely strike ye for the free.

For your help at our young struggle
When fair Freedom's war was won,
Glows the spirit of the father
Grateful living in the son.

For the ties of blood that bind us,
For the kin of blood we trace,
For the blood in veins of all men,
Here's for freedom and the race.

Hail, ye brothers! Hail, ye sisters!
Struggling for dear Freedom's right!
Take our hand—all men are brothers—
More we pledge you—FREEMEN'S MIGHT.

God has robed the world in beauty,
    Robed the land, the sea, the sky;
Bound are we in love and duty—
    You and I, you and I.

God commands to love each other
    As our work we daily ply;
Here's my hand, my sister, brother—
    You and I, you and I.

We shall live and toil together,
    And our daily wants supply;
But we'll spurn the lightest tether—
    You and I, you and I.

Freedom's banner, all-enfolding,
    Freedom's rights to glorify.
Hold we up to all beholding—
    You and I, you and I.

Blessed is the lot of labor
    When its strokes in love we ply;
Each is every other's neighbor—
    You and I, you and I.

LECHER BALDWIN.

It may be asked why this poem is found among "Labor Rhymes." The subject of it, in addition to his beastliness, is the employer of three hundred coolies. It is well that other monopolists know in whose company they muster.

Besides, I think it better in morals as well as in manliness, to publish while its author may be made responsible, than to leave it to be some time hence given out posthumously.

My curse upon thee, " Lucky " man—
Thy crime too foul for tongue to name;
For ever be thou under ban,
The deep damnation of thy shame.

Right glad we seek in vain to find,
In human story, thing so base—
Thou miscreate that mocks our kind
With biped semblance of the race!

I've named thee man; thou art not such;
'Twould libel beasts to call thee beast;
The reptiles vile in filth that slutch,
Would nauseate turn from thy foul feast.

Of all the things that creep or crawl
    Upon their bellies on the earth—
Of vipers, scorpions, adders all—
    Thou art than they of lower worth.

Our mother tongue has never heard
    For thing so foul as thee a name;
Let *Lecher* Baldwin be that word
    To synonym thy crime and shame.

'Tis Lecher Baldwin, while there lives
    On earth, as thou, so foul a blot;
When none of thee or thine survives,
    Be it and thou alike forgot.

I pity thee, poor miscreate
    With soul so shriveled, dwarfed and vile,
So low that no thing animate
    Can touch thy hand without defile.

As man, henceforth, we know thee not,
    Go wallow in thy slimy den;
As lecher vile, thou art boycott
    In all the walks and ways of men.

For all thy foul, unnaméd crimes,
    For all thy words and ways obscene,
As lepers were in olden times,
    We bid, begone! Unclean! Unclean!

Thou worst abort of woman born,
  Henceforth a by-word and a hiss;
The cat-o'-nine-tails of our scorn
  Shall be thy 'venging Nemesis.

A bright day is coming
  In sunshine and beauty—
The day for the toiling
To bless them forever.
When honor shall come as
  The guerdon of duty—
    Work on, hope ever.

But let not your thoughts be
  An idle bewailing—
A fruitless imploring
Your fetters to sever;
But stand ye for freedom
  With spirit unquailing—
    Work on, hope ever.

For never can conquer
  The Right, but by trying—
Unyielding must be our
Unchanging endeavor:

The truth be proclaiming
And error defying—
    Work on, hope ever.

For not can conviction
    Be carried by pleading—
Nor stony hearts melted
When wooed as a lover—
Come on in your numbers
    Where Honor is leading—
        Work on, hope ever.

The day that is coming
    Is glory to labor,
With justice unswerving
A ruler for ever,
When kindness and love shall
    Own each as a neighbor—
        Work on, hope ever.

The flag of the fathers
    Shall wave in its glory,
And freedom be real—
A blessing for ever—
And all shall rejoice as
    They're learning the story—
        Work on, hope ever.

THE BETTER FOR THE DOING.

Droop not! though shame, sin and anguish are
   'round thee!
Bravely fling off the cold chain that hath bound
   thee!
Look to the pure heaven smiling beyond thee!
   Rest not content in thy darkness—a clod!
Work for some good, be it ever so slowly!
Cherish some flower, be it ever so lowly!
Labor! all labor is noble and holy!
   Let thy great deed be thy prayer to thy God!
               —FRANCIS S. OSGOOD.

Through the dim twilight of the ages—
   From cycles, long ago, of time—
Still come the voices of the sages;
And written on historic pages
   Are names of men of deed sublime.

The world doth joy, the world doth glory
  In its great names of long ago—
The demigods of ancient story,
  Who waked mankind from sin and woe—
  Whose deeds it is our school to know.

Arouse thee, O my laggard spirit,
  Let deed of greatness then be thine,
And bless the world that shall inherit
  Thy name, thy fame, thy great design
  In word, or deed, or living line.

If on thy name wouldst have no blackness,
  No spot of foulness mar thy fame,
Then in thy work must be no slackness;
  Thy soul must glow, a living flame,
  Undimmed by aught of sin or shame.

Think'st thou there is no living Hydra?
  No monster in thy path to-day?
Ah! cleanse thou yon Augean stable,
And yon Procrustean tyrant slay—
  Where all must walk, make clear the way.

Seest Mammon's sons at their devotions?
  Before their sordid god they fall;
They know not pity's pure emotions,
  Nor thought above the things that crawl—
  But human reptiles are they all.

Seest thou the wrong vile Mammon's doing—
  Debasing Labor to a slave—
The work the fathers did undoing—
  Despoiling all the gifts they gave,
  And dragging Freedom to the grave?

Throughout the years have maundered, driveled
  These Mammon's greedy devotees—
These sightless souls so dwarfed and shriveled—
  Like things called animalcules
  That eye microscopic sees.

See yonder banner won by freemen—
  Shall it o'er aught than freemen wave?
Shall pale its stars in sight of heaven?
  Wilt spurn the gifts the fathers gave
  And own thyself a cringing slave?

Or wilt thou yield, a crawling, creeping—
  A craven, over-burdened drudge?
Is this the harvest for our reaping?
  Know, who for masters willing trudge
  Shall wallow in the dirt and sludge.

Strike down the power all enslaving,
  Hold up the banner of the free,
O'er land of Freedom proudly waving;
  And Freedom's land it e'er shall be,
  Where none to tyrant bows the knee.

What is the reason—dost thou ask me,
    O laggard spirit of my life,
Why to thy utmost strength I task thee—
    Why struggle in the scenes of strife,
    With turmoil, toil and danger rife?

I answer that thou art a human
    With soul to dare and hand to do;
For who aspires to be a true man,
    Must labor on his journey through
    And bid to ease and sloth adieu.

Thou might'st beneath the weeping willow
    On flowery beds of ease recline,
And idly dream upon thy pillow
    Of goblets red with flowing wine—
    Thy hours to useless ease resign.

Thou might'st, I grant, with little labor,
    Contrive to know what others know,
As wise become as is thy neighbor,
    And do, perchance, as others do!
    With idlesse all the journey through.

Doth love of man or hope of heaven
    My laggard spirit e'er inspire?
For every talent God has given,
    Know, ten will be of thee require,
    All cleansed and purified by fire.

'Tis work that strength the toiler gives,
  For all he does, he gains the more;
And struggling on each day he lives
    Is better for the day before,
    And wiser for its garnered lore.

It is the law of human growing,
  We stronger are for what we do;
And whether brain or brawn bestowing,
    The power that's spent doth power renew—
    We truer grow for being true.

From day to day the strength grows stronger,
  Is greatened by the work that's done,
And life itself, protracted longer,
    Is youthful to its setting sun,
    And cheerful for its triumphs won.

The sailor on the wide, wild ocean,
  As oft by storm-fiend haply spared—
The soldier used to war's commotion,
    Who fields of death has bravely shared,
    More daring is for dangers dared.

And he who watches the careering
  Of planets through the realms on high,
But sees the farther for this peering
    Of his heaven-searching eye,
    To solve the problems of the sky.

The mind is greatened by its thinking,
   With better fiber builds the brain;
The thought-pulse quickens by this linking
   Of truth to truth, an endless chain
   Uniting Reason's wide domain.

And so is, too, the power of loving—
   We better love for love we bear,
And every deed of heart-felt kindness
   But lifts us up where angels are,
   The sweetness of their peace to share.

If in each work that's worth the doing,
   To well do be the golden rule,
In the vocation we're pursuing,
   We'll find life's labor is a school—
   To higher life the vestibule.

And praising God for work that's given
   From morning dawn to set of sun,
The stronger be that we have striven,
   The better for the work that's done
   And greater for the glories won.

All noble thought and noble feeling
   Must ever make the soul more pure,
And each day's toil the truth's revealing
   That God doth bless the noble doer
   And on to greater works allure.

Then hail! my brother! hail! my sister!
  Toiling on life's rugged way;
For ye shall reap in the hereafter
  Rich blessings for the toils to-day.